To Ann
It "brightens"
my spirit
to be
around you!

Jai Gill

Dedicated to:

To Shannon, my little flower

HATS

© copyright 1998 by ARO Publishing.
All rights reserved, including the right of reproduction in whole or
in part in any form. Designed and produced by ARO Publishing.
Printed in the U.S.A. P.O. Box 193 Provo, Utah 84603

ISBN 0-89868-348-3–Library Bound
ISBN 0-89868-407-2–Soft Bound
ISBN 0-89868-349-1–Trade

A PREDICTABLE WORD BOOK

HATS

Story by Janie Spaht Gill, Ph.D.
Illustrations by Elizabeth Lambson

ARO PUBLISHING

4

Which hat is right for
the party tonight . . .

my droopy hat,

8

my silly hat,

my fancy or my frilly hat,

11

12

my rain hat,

my sun hat,

my Halloween fun hat,

my big hat,

or small hat,

my black, shiny, tall hat?

21

22

I can't pick one, so instead,
I'll stack them all upon my
head.